My
Church History
Storybook

MY CHURCH HISTORY STORYBOOK
IS PRESENTED TO:

_____

ON THIS DATE:

_____

PRESENTED BY:

_____

My Church History Storybook

As Told and Illustrated by
Laura Lee Rostrom

Author's Note: This book contains quotes from various sources. They
are characterized in *italic* print and the source is given at the end of
the chapter.

This book is not an official publication of The Church of Jesus Christ of
Latter-day Saints.

ISBN: 1-55517-698-4

10 9 8 7 6 5 4 3 2 1

Published and distributed by:

Typeset by Marny K. Parkin

Library of Congress Control Number: 2003106311

Printed in Korea

ACKNOWLEDGMENTS

A warm thank you to my "editors" Alexa Hiatt, Beth Hiatt, Dan Hiatt, Joyce Thompson, Amanda Rostrom, Dean Rostrom and the Cedar Fort team. Thank you to my "art directors," Ryan Rostrom (his animals are on pages 16, 59, 126, 154, 177, 196, 206 and 237) and Sean Rostrom (his waves are on page 174).

I'm grateful to my "historians," who collected and shared their special pioneer stories. Millie Lewis' stories are *Noah Brimhall, Praying for Rain, Settling Arizona, William Walker* and *The Little Bible.* Beth Hiatt shared *The Mormon Battalion* and *Abraham Hunsaker.* And thank you to my mother, Betty Lee Harrison Blocher, for her continued support and to my father, Loren Milam Blocher, for sharing his personal stories, *A Little Voice* and *Joy to the World.*

I was deeply touched by all of the miracles that happened during this time period. I believe the people in these stories really lived and that the miracles really happened. These people suffered so much individually, and yet as a group, they prevailed.

This book is dedicated to pioneers,
both past and present—you know who you are!

God bless you!

CONTENTS

JOSEPH SMITH
23 DECEMBER 1805

On a cold Vermont winter day in 1805, a baby boy was born. His parents, Joseph Smith Sr. and Lucy Mack Smith, were very happy to have another son. They named him Joseph Smith Jr.

Joseph liked helping his father on their
farm. In the spring, they planted corn
and beans and other crops. In the fall,
they picked the fruits and vegetables that
grew during the summer. When their
farm did not grow crops very well in
Vermont, they moved to Palmyra,
New York.

Joseph's three sisters and four brothers helped their mother and father on their farm. Joseph especially liked working and playing with his older brother, Hyrum. Hyrum was five years older than Joseph and they were very good friends.

JOSEPH'S COURAGE

One day when Joseph was seven years old, he came down with a terrible illness. It was called typhoid fever. He felt pain all through his left leg. After a few weeks, he could hardly bear the pain. Sometimes Hyrum helped by holding on tight to his brother's sore leg. This made Joseph feel better.

After several weeks, Joseph's parents
sent for a doctor. The doctor said he
needed to operate on his left leg. The
surgeon wanted to tie Joseph to the bed
during the surgery, but Joseph did not
like that idea. He told the doctor that he
could control his arms himself.

Then the doctor suggested he drink
some brandy or wine. The doctor knew
Joseph would feel a lot of pain during
the operation. The alcohol would lessen
the pain.

But Joseph said, "I will not touch one particle of liquor, neither will I be tied down; but I will tell you what I will do—I will have my father sit on the bed and hold me in his arms, and then I will do whatever is necessary in order to have the bone taken out."

And to his mother, Joseph said, "Mother, I want you to leave the room, for I know you cannot bear to see me suffer so. . . . Promise me that you will not stay. Will you? The Lord will help me and I shall get through with it."

At his request, Joseph's mother left the room. Then his father hugged him tight and the doctor started the operation. The doctor cut into Joseph's infected leg and carved away bone. Joseph only cried out one time.

After the infected bone was removed, Joseph started feeling better. Soon he could run and play just like the other children. His family was so glad to see him feeling well and happy.

Lucy Mack Smith,
History of Joseph Smith, 55–58

JOSEPH'S FAITH

While living in Palmyra, New York, Joseph felt that he should join one of the many churches in town.

His mother and two brothers and one sister went to one church, and his father and his other brothers went to a different church. Each Sunday, the preachers called out to the people asking them to come join their church. The preachers each said all the other churches were wrong.

Joseph Smith was fourteen years old. He
was very confused about which church
to join. Sometimes he went to church
with his mother and other times he
went with his father.

James 1:5
If any of you lack wisdom,
let him ask of God, that
giveth to all men liberally,
and upbraideth not;
and it shall be given him.

One day, Joseph was reading from the Bible. In James 1:5 he read, *"If any of you lack wisdom, let him ask of God, that giveth to all men liberally, and upbraideth not; and it shall be given him."*

Joseph thought about this scripture. To him, this meant that if he prayed and asked which church to join and had faith, then God would answer his prayer. So Joseph decided to pray to God and ask which church he should join.

James 1:5

THE FIRST VISION
1820

On a lovely spring morning, Joseph walked outside to a quiet grove of trees to pray. Here he had lots of privacy. Joseph knelt down and started to pray out loud. At first he felt strange. He could not see around him and it was hard to talk. Then suddenly the darkness left and Joseph could talk again. He felt much better.

Then Joseph saw two personages coming out of heaven towards him. Heavenly Father spoke to Joseph. He said, *"This is My Beloved Son. Hear Him!"* Joseph asked Jesus Christ which church to join. Jesus told Joseph not to join any of the churches. He said that people had changed His true teachings. He wanted Joseph to restore the true gospel of Jesus Christ.

Joseph was surprised! This was not the answer he expected. But he was relieved to finally know the truth. Joseph told his family that he saw Heavenly Father and Jesus Christ. His family knew Joseph well. They knew he was honest. They believed and supported him.

Joseph Smith—History 1:17

ANGRY!

Joseph told the local preachers that he saw Heavenly Father and Jesus Christ. Until now, the preachers all liked Joseph, but they did not like the idea of him seeing a vision. After Joseph told them about his vision, they were mean to him. They were very angry with Joseph!

Nearly all of the people in Palmyra heard about Joseph's vision. Some of the people thought he was just making up the story. Others thought he was crazy. After all, it's not everyday that someone claims to see God.

But the people close to Joseph believed him. They knew he was honest. They saw his faithfulness and knew he was a good young man. They supported him and stood by him during this difficult time.

MORONI'S VISIT
1823

Three years later, when Joseph was seventeen, he knelt to say a special prayer. He asked Heavenly Father to forgive him for all his childhood sins. An angel appeared to him later that evening. The angel's name was Moroni and the Lord had sent him. Moroni would teach Joseph many important things.

Moroni said that Joseph would do great
things. He said that someday he would
translate an ancient record and it would
be a very important book for the whole
world.

Moroni left Joseph for a while but then came back two more times during the night. The next day, Moroni came one more time. He showed Joseph where to find the ancient golden plates. They were buried in a hill a few miles from Joseph's home.

Joseph went to the Hill Cumorah. On the hill, Joseph saw a large stone that was rounded on top. The edges were covered with dirt. Joseph cleared off the dirt and moved the stone. The stone covered a stone box. Inside the box were items left by Moroni over one thousand years ago.

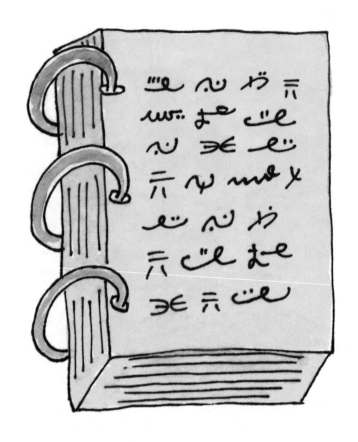

Inside the box, Joseph saw golden plates. The plates were held together with three rings. The writing on the plates looked strange to Joseph. He also saw a breastplate and an Urim and Thummim. Moroni explained to Joseph that he would use the Urim and Thummim to translate the plates at a later time.

Moroni asked Joseph to visit this spot
every year on the same day. Moroni
wanted to meet Joseph and teach him.
Someday, the Lord would have Joseph
take the plates from the stone box and
translate them.

THE GOLDEN PLATES
1827

A few years later, Joseph met a young woman named Emma Hale. Emma was very nice and they fell in love. Joseph asked Emma to marry him. It was a happy day for the young couple. Shortly after they married, Moroni visited Joseph again and told him that it was time to translate the plates.

Joseph and Emma rode to the Hill
Cumorah together. Emma waited for
Joseph while he climbed the hill. It was
late September and the weather was
probably warm and pleasant.

Joseph climbed the hill and found the round stone. He removed the stone and took out the golden plates and the Urim and Thummim. Then he carried the ancient items down the hill. Emma was waiting for him.

Joseph and Emma returned to their
home with the golden plates.
Unfortunately, there were some mean
men living in Joseph's town. They heard
about the golden plates and they wanted
to steal them. If they could melt down
the gold, they would be rich! They tried
to break into Joseph and Emma's home
many times.

Joseph and Emma were scared and
decided to move. They did not feel safe
living in Palmyra anymore. They moved
to Harmony, Pennsylvania. They stayed
with Emma's father, Isaac Hale.

TRANSLATING THE GOLDEN PLATES
1828–29

Emma was a great help to Joseph. He used the Urim and Thummim to translate the ancient plates. Often, Emma helped by writing down what Joseph read from the plates.

Joseph had two close friends named
Martin Harris and Oliver Cowdery. They
also helped Joseph during this time.
Oliver Cowdery described this time with
Joseph as one he would always
remember. He said, *"To sit under the
sound of a voice dictated by the
inspiration of heaven, awakened the
utmost gratitude of this bosom!"*

Joseph and Oliver were so busy translating the plates into English that they forgot to do anything else. One day, they realized that they were out of supplies, even food. They went into town looking for work, but they could not find a job anywhere. They walked home hungry and discouraged.

However, to their pleasant surprise, they saw an old friend waiting for them. It was Joseph Knight Sr. He had heard Joseph needed help. He brought lined paper, a barrel of fish, several bushels of grain and potatoes. Joseph and Oliver were so glad. Now they had food and supplies to last until they finished translating the plates.

Joseph Smith—History 1:71, footnote

THE BOOK OF MORMON

While translating the plates, Joseph learned so much. The golden plates taught about an ancient people. It told of a family traveling from Jerusalem to the American Continent. The family later divided into two groups. They called themselves Lamanites and Nephites.

Nephite prophets kept records of their
history and wrote of important events.
The Nephites knew about Jesus Christ.
The angel Moroni, who visited Joseph
Smith, was a Nephite prophet. He was
the last person to write on the golden
plates. He buried them in the Hill
Cumorah.

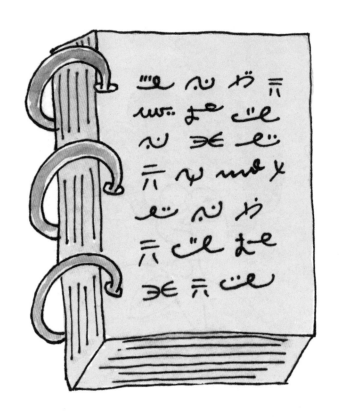

Mormon was Moroni's father. He was a great man and a prophet of God. Mormon had numerous plates passed down to him. He took the most important writings and wrote them on the golden plates. This was a lot of work. When Mormon was finished writing he gave the plates to his son, Moroni. Because Mormon rewrote these writings for us to have in one book, the plates are called The Book of Mormon.

TWELVE WITNESSES
1829

One day when Joseph was translating the plates, he read that there would be other witnesses who would see the golden plates. A witness is a person who sees something with his own eyes. There were three men who asked Joseph if they could be the special witnesses.

Joseph and the three men went into a
quiet grove of trees to pray, but their
prayers were not answered. After
praying twice, one of the men stood up
and left. His name was Martin Harris. He
went to pray alone. He did not think that
he was worthy to see the plates. He
thought it was because of him that their
prayers were not answered.

After he left, Joseph and the other two men started to pray. Soon the angel Moroni appeared. He showed the golden plates to Oliver Cowdery and David Whitmer. They heard a voice from above. It said that Joseph Smith translated the plates and that the teachings were true. The voice told the men to tell people what they saw that day.

After this vision, Joseph found Martin Harris. Together, they knelt and started to pray. Soon Joseph saw and heard the same vision. Joseph wondered if Martin could see the plates. Soon, Martin called out in joy, "*'Tis enough; 'tis enough; mine eyes have beheld; mine eyes have beheld.*"

Later, Joseph showed the golden plates to eight other men. The men held the plates in their own hands. They wrote a testimony of what they saw. Their testimonies are still found today at the front of every Book of Mormon.

Joseph was so grateful to have other witnesses. For a while he was the only one to see the golden plates. Many people thought he was lying. But now he had eleven other witnesses to defend him and the Book of Mormon.

History of the Church, 1:54–55

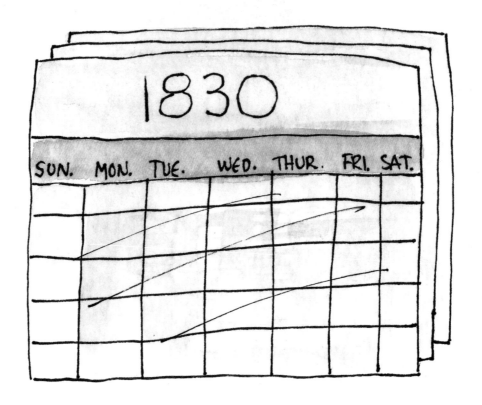

THE FIRST PRINTING
26 MARCH 1830

Joseph finished translating the plates in two months. This was truly a miracle! Joseph did not have much schooling and greedy men kept trying to steal the plates. But Joseph was able to quickly complete the Lord's work.

Other miracles happened during this time, too. Joseph needed a lot of money to print the Book of Mormon. He needed 3,000 dollars. He did not have any money to pay for it so kind people helped him. He was able to get all of the money he needed.

Also, many publishers did not want to print this book, but he found one publisher in Palmyra, New York, who agreed to print it. This was wonderful news!

The publisher had a brand new printing press. It was the best press made at the time. It printed more copies at once than other printers, so the printing went very fast. They printed 5,000 copies. The Book of Mormon was now ready for all to read.

THE PRIESTHOOD
1829

Along with translating the Book of Mormon, Jesus wanted Joseph to organize Jesus Christ's church on the earth. On May 15, 1829, an angel visited Joseph and Oliver. The angel was John the Baptist. He placed his hands on their heads and gave them the Aaronic Priesthood. The angel also gave Joseph and Oliver the authority to baptize.

Later, three more angels came to visit
them. They were Peter, James and John.
The angels were apostles of Jesus when
He lived on the earth. They gave Joseph
and Oliver the Melchizedek Priesthood.

This was a very important time. Now Joseph had the authority to baptize people and he could start Jesus Christ's church on the earth.

April 6, 1830

THE CHURCH OF JESUS CHRIST OF LATTER-DAY SAINTS
6 APRIL 1830

The Lord asked Joseph Smith to organize His church. Notices were given out to friends and family. Fifty-six men, women and children came to the cabin of Peter Whitmer Sr. He lived in Fayette, New York. The people were very excited. Joseph chose six men to help organize Jesus Christ's church.

Joseph started the meeting with a prayer.
Then he asked if everyone accepted
Joseph as their teacher. All agreed.

All agreed that they should organize The
Church of Jesus Christ. Then Oliver and
Joseph ordained each other as Elders.
Those people who had been baptized
earlier were given the gift of the Holy
Ghost. The people rejoiced. This was
such a happy day!

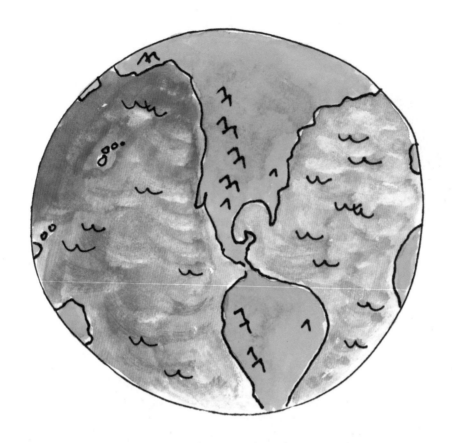

Joseph said, "*It is only a little handful of priesthood you see here tonight, but this Church will fill North and South America. It will fill the Rocky Mountains.*" Joseph called the church, The Church of Jesus Christ of Latter-day Saints since the Church is led by Jesus. They called each other Saints like the Saints who followed Jesus when He was on the earth.

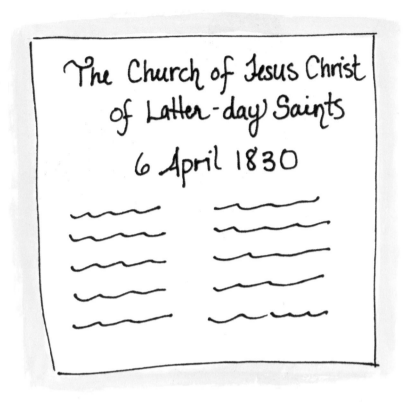

The Church of Jesus Christ
of Latter-day Saints

6 April 1830

Joseph Smith's entire family was baptized and joined the Church. They believed that Joseph was a prophet of God. They and the new Church members were grateful for the restored gospel.

Presidents of the Church,
Student Manual Religion 345
(Salt Lake City: The Church of Jesus Christ of Latter-day Saints, 1972), 34

TROUBLE IN COLESVILLE

After organizing the Church, Joseph left on a mission. He traveled to Colesville, New York, to teach his friend, Joseph Knight Sr. The Knight family was happy to see Joseph. They listened to his message. They believed The Book of Mormon was true, and they wanted to be baptized.

Joseph and the Knight family found a
small river. They collected rocks and
branches and made a dam. As the water
started to collect to make a pool, some
mean men came and broke the dam.
They did not want anyone in Colesville
getting baptized into this new religion.

However, Joseph and the Knight family soon fixed the dam. Then the Knight family and several friends were baptized.

Joseph Knight Jr. wrote, "That night our wagons were turned over and wood piled on them, and some sunk in the water, rails were piled against our doors, and chains sunk in the stream and a great deal of mischief done."

The same people who broke the dam
told the police to arrest Joseph Smith.
They said he was making trouble. But
Joseph did not disturb anyone. The
Knights hired a lawyer and the police let
Joseph go.

The Knight family and their friends knew it would not always be easy being a member of Christ's church. But they believed it was true and were happy that they had the gospel.

Joseph Knight Autobiographical Sketch, 1862, in LDS Church Archives

TEACHING THE INDIANS

A few months later, four other Church members went on missions. Oliver Cowdery, Peter Whitmer Jr., Parley P. Pratt and Ziba Peterson were instructed to teach the Native Americans living in the area.

First, the four men traveled to Buffalo,
New York. Here they met with the
Cattaraugus Indians. They told them
about The Book of Mormon. The Book
of Mormon contains a history of their
people.

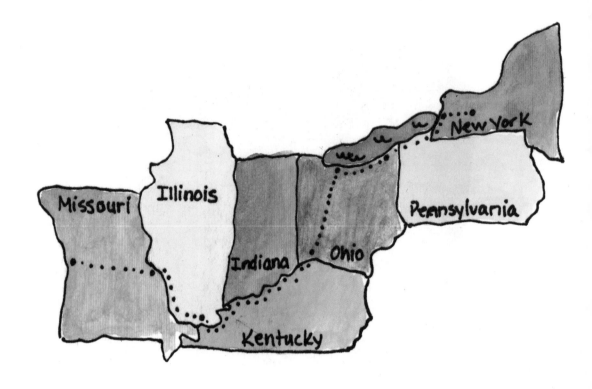

Next they traveled hundreds of miles
away to Ohio and beyond Missouri.
They taught the Wyandots and the
Delaware Indians. It was a very hard
mission. The missionaries were often
wet and freezing cold and they had to
sleep on the hard ground. But they did
their best to teach the gospel.

In Kirtland, Ohio, the missionaries met
some settlers. Here they taught the
gospel and it is just what the people
were waiting for. The missionaries
baptized 127 people in that area. After
the four missionaries left, the new
Church members shared the gospel with
their friends and neighbors. Soon, even
more people joined the Church.

LEAVING NEW YORK
1831

A new Church member living near Kirtland, Ohio, wanted to meet Joseph Smith. His name was Sidney Rigdon. He was a minister in another church before being baptized. He and his friend, Edward Partridge, wanted to learn more about the Church.

The two men went all the way from Ohio
to New York. They traveled over 250
miles to see Joseph Smith. The Prophet
was grateful to hear about the new
Church members in Ohio. Joseph prayed
to Heavenly Father for further guidance.

The Lord answered Joseph's prayer. He told Joseph to gather the Church members in New York and move to Ohio.

CROSSING LAKE ERIE

The Church members living in Colesville, Fayette and Manchester, New York prepared to move to Ohio. They wanted to follow the Prophet Joseph Smith and obey the Lord's command. The people had to quickly sell their homes, farms and property before they could leave.

Lucy Mack Smith, Joseph's mother, helped organize the move out of Fayette. Over eighty Church members left Fayette and traveled to Lake Erie. Everyone was very excited to sail to Ohio. They boarded a steamboat and patiently waited to leave.

Unfortunately, the lake was freezing over. The boat could not move if the lake was frozen. Their excitement soon turned to disappointment, but Lucy had faith in God. She asked all the Church members to pray and they asked the Lord to break the ice. She said, *"Sure as the Lord lives, it will be done."*

At the moment she said this everyone heard a loud cracking noise. The ice had broken apart! They set off quickly and moved away from the frozen port. After they left the harbor, they looked back and saw the water freeze over again. What a miracle! The Church members came together and prayed. They thanked the Lord for hearing and answering their prayers.

Lucy Mack Smith,
History of Joseph Smith, *204*

THE DOCTRINE AND COVENANTS

The Church members living in Ohio welcomed the members from New York. Many of the new members stayed in Ohio, others moved on to Missouri. It was a time for spiritual growth and Joseph Smith received many revelations from the Lord.

Joseph wrote down the revelations and called them The Book of Commandments. Joseph wanted to print them into a book. A printer, who was a member of the Church in Missouri, was preparing to print them when trouble broke out. One day, an angry mob stormed the printing shop.

Two young sisters, Elizabeth and
Caroline Rollins, heard the mob yelling,
"Here are the Mormon Commandments."
Then they saw the mob throwing the
unbound pages into the street. The young
sisters decided to save the papers.

The two sisters ran to the street. They grabbed as many pages as they could hold. The men from the mob saw them and shouted for them to stop. The girls ran away as fast as they could. The angry men ran after them.

The girls quickly moved into a tall field of corn and hid from the mean men. They laid the papers on the ground and sat on top of them. The angry men looked all through the cornfield but could not find the girls. The papers and the girls were safe!

Soon the saved pages were published into a book. Later the book's name was changed to The Doctrine and Covenants. The Doctrine and Covenants is still used today by Church members, thanks to Elizabeth and Caroline!

OUR HERITAGE: A Brief History of The Church of Jesus Christ of Latter-day Saints, 41

THE WORD OF WISDOM
1833

A special revelation given to Joseph Smith is known as The Word of Wisdom. Joseph Smith's wife, Emma, did not like the smoke that lingered after meetings held by her husband. She complained to Joseph. He agreed that the smoke was annoying. He asked the Lord about this matter.

The Lord answered with a revelation. He told Joseph that tobacco, alcoholic drinks and hot drinks are not good for our bodies. He said we should eat fruits, vegetables and whole grains, like bread. He said we should take care of our animals and eat just a little meat.

The people who obey the Word of Wisdom and live the commandments are given a promise. They "*shall receive health . . . and run and not be weary, and shall walk and not faint.*" They will live a long and healthy life.

D&C 89:18, 20

THE FIRST HYMN BOOK
1835

The Lord told Joseph many important things. He once said, "*For my soul delighteth in the song of the heart; yea, the song of the righteous is a prayer unto me, and it shall be answered with a blessing upon their heads.*" When Joseph heard this, he asked his wife Emma for help.

Joseph asked Emma to collect her favorite hymns. After she collected a variety of hymns they were published in a hymn book. Every Sunday, the Church members used the songbooks to sing their favorite songs. They also memorized many of the songs and they sang them while working and playing. Today Church members still sing the hymns Emma collected.

D&C 25:12

THE KIRTLAND TEMPLE
1833–36

The Lord asked the Saints to build a temple. A temple is different than a regular church building. A temple is a special place to do God's work. Constructing a temple was a huge sacrifice. Most of the Church members were poor. But after three years of hard work they completed the beautiful Kirtland Temple.

It was a joyous time! Over one thousand Saints came to celebrate and give thanks to the Lord. William W. Phelps wrote a special song called *The Spirit of God*. The crowd joyfully sang this new hymn. It was a very special day for the Saints.

MISSIONARIES GO FORTH
1832

Many of the Saints that came to Kirtland were soon asked to travel and serve on missions. The Lord told Joseph, *"Ye shall go forth in the power of my Spirit, preaching my gospel, two by two, in my name, lifting up your voices as with the sound of a trump, declaring my work like unto angels of God."*

Many men served missions. The
missionaries shared the restored gospel
with lots of people. It was not always
easy for them. The missionaries had to
leave their families and walk in the cold
and rain. But the Lord blessed the
missionaries and they were happy.

Two men who served missions were
Zerah Pulsipher and Elijah Cheney. They
traveled to Richland, New York, and
baptized several people.

One of the men that they baptized was named Wilford Woodruff. He was a young farmer. Wilford joined the Church and later served a mission himself. Zera and Elijah probably did not know that this young farmer would someday become a great Church leader. Later, Wilford Woodruff became the fourth prophet of the Church.

D&C 42:6

ELDER PAGE

There were all kinds of missionaries. Some were single men. Some were married men with children. Some were young and some were old men, and some were very poor.

One man who wanted to serve a
mission was named Elder Page. But he
told Joseph Smith that he could not go
because he did not have a coat to wear.
The Prophet then took off his own coat
and gave it to Elder Page.

Joseph told Elder Page that he could
now serve a mission and the Lord would
bless him. The man took the coat and
went on a mission. He was blessed and
touched the lives of hundreds of people
who joined the Church.

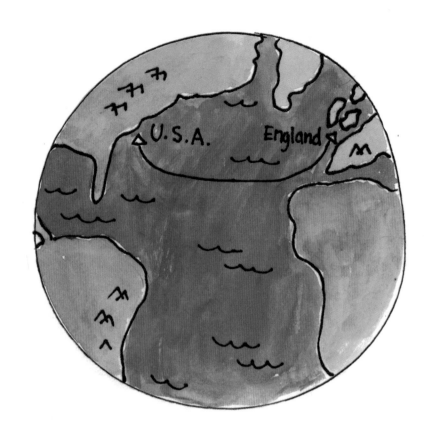

EXCITEMENT IN ENGLAND
1837

Joseph Smith was inspired to send missionaries to England. England was far away from Kirtland, Ohio. Missionaries had to travel by ship for many weeks. But Heber C. Kimball and Orson Hyde gladly accepted this mission call.

Orson Hyde and Heber C. Kimball were
very excited the day they sailed into
England. Orson leaped off the ship
shouting that he was the first to arrive in
England with the restored gospel! Soon,
Orson and Heber were teaching many
people. Overflowing crowds listened to
what the missionaries taught and many
were grateful to hear the gospel.

They scheduled the first baptisms and
the people were truly excited. Everyone
wanted to be the first baptized but only
one could go first. To choose who would
be baptized first, they held a footrace.
Whoever won the footrace would be the
first baptized.

The people lined up. Someone shouted, "*GO!*" and a group of people took off running. George D. Watt crossed the finish line first and won the race. He was the first person baptized in England. It was a very happy time for the missionaries and for the new members.

Orson F. Whitney, Life of Heber C. Kimball, *3rd ed. (1945), 104*

MISSOURI
JUNE 1834

While some Church members gathered to live in Kirtland, Ohio, another group moved on to live in Missouri. This was a very difficult time for the Saints. The people already living in Missouri did not welcome the "Mormons."

Large groups of angry men formed
together into mobs. The mobs did
terrible things to the Saints. The Church
members had to defend themselves.

Once a mob fired cannon balls at Joseph
Smith and other Church members.
Joseph wondered how they would
protect themselves, but soon low, heavy
clouds covered the sky. It began to rain,
hail and thunder. A huge rainstorm
started to pour down on them.

The mob stopped firing at the Church
members because of the violent storm.
When the rain stopped, all of the mob's
weapons were wet. They could not
fight any more. Joseph was so grateful.
The Lord had protected them.

AMANDA'S FAITH
30 OCTOBER 1838

In Missouri, people were often mean to the Church members. It was such a hard time for them. But with hardships also came miracles.

The Governor of Missouri, Lilburn W. Boggs, did not like the Mormons. He wrote an extermination order in October 1838. It said that all Mormons had to leave the state of Missouri. If they did not leave, the militia had orders to kill them.

Three days later in late October, a mob
of two hundred men surprised a group
of Church members living in a town
called Haun's Mill. The mob tricked the
men by telling them to go inside the
blacksmith shop to be safe. But as soon
as the men were inside the shop, the
mob started shooting at the building.

Most of the men and boys died. It was such a sad day. After the mob left, the women went inside the building to find their loved ones.

Amanda Smith was one of the women. She lost her husband and one son in the shooting, but she found her seven-year-old son still alive. His name was Alma. He was hit in the hip and was bleeding. Amanda cried out pleading, *Heavenly Father direct me what to do!* Then she heard a soft voice telling her how to care for his hip.

She prepared herbs and a wrap to put on his hip. Then she laid him on his stomach in a special way. After five weeks, Alma was completely healed! Amanda was truly thankful. The Lord had heard and answered her prayer.

Amanda Barnes Smith, quoted in Tullidge, Women of Mormondom, *126*

BENJAMIN'S MIRACLE
1838

A miracle also happened to a Church member named Benjamin F. Johnson. He was twenty years old when a mob of angry men captured him. Eight nights later Benjamin was sitting on a log outside in the bitter cold.

One of the men who captured Benjamin jumped up and yelled, *"You give up Mormonism right now, or I'll shoot you."* Benjamin refused. He could not give up his faith. Benjamin believed it was true. This made the man even angrier. He aimed his gun at Benjamin and pulled the trigger, but to his surprise, the gun did not go off.

The angry man said, "*Used the gun
20 years and it had never before missed
fire.*" He tried shooting at Benjamin again
and then again, but nothing happened.
Another man suggested that he fix his
gun. The angry man cleaned and
reloaded the gun and tried a fourth time.

This time, however, the whole gun blew up, killing the angry man. One of the men watching said to their group, *"You'd better not try to kill that man."* Benjamin was safe now. He was grateful for this miracle. This and other miracles helped the Saints through difficult times.

E. Dale LeBaron, "Benjamin Franklin Johnson: Colonizer, Public Servant, and Church Leader," 42–43

THE PROPHET JOSEPH SMITH
1838

The Prophet Joseph Smith and other leaders were treated cruelly by the mobs. State militia captured Joseph and they wanted to kill him, but the General in charge said that Joseph was not guilty of any crime. So he stopped the militia from hurting Joseph.

However, the militia held Joseph for six
months. He was jailed with another
Church member, Parley P. Pratt. One
night while they tried sleeping on the
cold, hard floor, the guards got out of
control.

They were using bad language and saying cruel things in front of the Prophet. They were also confessing to horrible things that they did to other Church members. Joseph could not listen any longer. Jumping up from the floor, he yelled out to the guards:

"SILENCE, ye fiends of the infernal pit. In the name of Jesus Christ I rebuke you, and command you to be still; I will not live another minute and hear such language. Cease such talk. Or you or I die THIS INSTANT!"

Joseph was chained and did not have a weapon, but the guards felt his power and greatness. Parley P. Pratt felt like he was in the presence of a great king. The guards dropped their weapons to the ground and they quietly moved away to a corner. Kneeling down, the guards said they were sorry and stayed quiet the rest of the night.

Autobiography of Parley P. Pratt, *211*

MOVING OUT
1838–39

After Missouri's governor wrote the extermination order, the Saints could no longer stay in Missouri. It was not safe. With their prophet Joseph still in jail, the Saints moved on without him. The people looked to Brigham Young and other Church leaders for guidance.

Over eight thousand Church members
moved from Missouri to Illinois. If life
was bad in Missouri, their move was
even worse. They packed what they
could and quickly left in the freezing cold
of winter.

Most of the people did not have proper clothes to wear for this move. One man said that only his mother and sister had shoes to wear in his family. And their shoes had worn out by the time they reached Illinois. Many people had to wrap their feet in cloth for protection. It was a very hard move for the Saints.

NAUVOO
1839

Shortly after the Saints left Missouri, the Prophet Joseph was released from jail. He found his family and friends in good health but needing lots of things. Joseph was so happy to be with his family and friends. The Church members enjoyed having Joseph with them. He worked and preached among them.

The Saints finally settled in Nauvoo,
Illinois. They were right next to the
Mississippi River. They felt safe here.
Soon they built homes and churches.
They also planted crops for food. Nauvoo
quickly became one of the largest cities
in Illinois.

In Nauvoo, the Church members felt at peace. They had food to eat and they could work freely. They could also worship as they pleased. For a little while, it would be a happy and prosperous time for the Church members.

THE NAUVOO TEMPLE

Joseph directed the Saints to build a temple. Joseph asked the men to give one day out of ten to work on the temple. Women helped by feeding the men, donating goods and collecting pennies and dimes. Even the women in far away England wanted to help. They gathered 50,000 pennies and shipped them to Nauvoo.

In Nauvoo, Caroline Butler did not have any pennies to give. She wondered how she could help. Then one day, she saw two dead buffaloes lying in a field. This gave her an idea of how she could help.

Caroline and her children started pulling
out the buffalo's mane. Then she made
heavy yarn with it. With the yarn, she
knitted eight pairs of warm mittens. She
donated the mittens to the men working
on the temple in the cold weather. She
felt good helping in this way.

The Church members worked very hard
and put their own needs last. Brigham
Young told the people that they should
work on the temple whenever they
could. He said the Lord would provide
food and other things that were needed.

A short time later, Joseph Toronto, a
new convert from Sicily, arrived in
Nauvoo. He had 2,500 dollars. He gave
all of his money to the Church leaders.
They purchased flour and other
supplies. Brigham Young was right. The
Lord provided for them. After three
years of hard work and sacrifice the
Nauvoo Temple was finally finished.

THE RELIEF SOCIETY
17 MARCH 1842

While the Nauvoo temple was being built, the women found different ways to help. Sarah Granger Kimball was one of the wealthiest people living in Nauvoo. She hired Margaret A. Cooke to sew her clothes. One day Sarah had an idea. She wanted to sew shirts for the men working on the temple.

Sarah bought bundles of fabric. Then her friend, Margaret, sewed shirts to give away to the men. Soon other women wanted to help. They met at Sarah's home and worked together. The women decided to join together and become a formal group.

One of the women, Eliza R. Snow, wrote
a special constitution. It described what
they wanted to do in their new group.
Eliza showed it to the Prophet.

Joseph Smith was impressed with Eliza's writing. He was also impressed that the women wanted to form a special group. Joseph thought about their constitution. He felt the women could do even more. He asked the women to come to a special meeting.

At the meeting, he organized the women
into the Nauvoo Female Relief Society.
His wife, Emma, was their first president.
The Relief Society's purpose was not just
to help others, but also to worship
together and to help build up Zion.

Their first project as a Relief Society was helping the poor. They collected money and goods to help people in need. They also made sure that all of the children could go to school. By collecting goods and money, they helped many people.

This organization still continues today. It is now called the Relief Society and it is the largest women's organization in the world. All female Church members eighteen years and older are welcome to join. They worship together and provide help and friendship to those who need it.

THE ARTICLES OF FAITH
1842

A man named John Wentworth once asked Joseph Smith what the Mormons believe in. Mr. Wentworth worked for a newspaper in Chicago, Illinois. Joseph Smith wrote him a letter. It is known as the Wentworth letter. In the letter, Joseph wrote about the history of the Church.

He also wrote a list of what the Church believes. This important list is known as the Articles of Faith. Mr. Wentworth did not publish the Articles of Faith, but the Church newspaper did. The Church members liked how the Articles of Faith explained their beliefs. Joseph Smith wrote:

1. We believe in God, the Eternal Father, and in His Son, Jesus Christ, and in the Holy Ghost.

2. We believe that men will be punished for their own sins, and not for Adam's transgression.

3. We believe that through the Atonement of Christ, all mankind may be saved, by obedience to the laws and ordinances of the Gospel.

4. We believe that the first principles and ordinances of the Gospel are: first, Faith in the Lord Jesus Christ; second, Repentance; third, Baptism by immersion for the remission of sins; fourth, Laying on of hands for the gift of the Holy Ghost.

5. We believe that a man must be called of God, by prophecy, and by the laying on of hands by those who are in authority, to preach the Gospel and administer in the ordinances thereof.

6. We believe in the same organization that existed in the Primitive Church, namely, apostles, prophets, pastors, teachers, evangelists, and so forth.

7. We believe in the gift of tongues, prophecy, revelation, visions, healing, interpretation of tongues, and so forth.

8. We believe the Bible to be the word of God as far as it is translated correctly; we also believe the Book of Mormon to be the word of God.

9. We believe all that God has revealed, all that He does now reveal, and we believe that He will

yet reveal many great and important things pertaining to the Kingdom of God.

10. We believe in the literal gathering of Israel and in the restoration of the Ten Tribes; that Zion (the New Jerusalem) will be built upon the American continent; that Christ will reign personally upon the earth; and, that the earth will be renewed and receive its paradisiacal glory.

11. We claim the privilege of worshiping Almighty God according to the dictates of our own conscience, and allow all men the same privilege, let them worship how, where, or what they may.

12. We believe in being subject to kings, presidents, rulers, and magistrates, in obeying, honoring, and sustaining the law.

13. We believe in being honest, true, chaste, benevolent, virtuous, and in doing good to all men; indeed, we may say that we follow the admonition of Paul—We believe all things, we hope all things, we have endured many things, and hope to be able to endure all things. If there is anything virtuous, lovely, or of good report or praiseworthy, we seek after these things.

Joseph Smith

The Articles of Faith 1–13

THE PEARL OF GREAT PRICE

Around this time Joseph Smith compiled an important book. It is called The Pearl of Great Price. Writings from the ancient prophets, Moses and Abraham, are in the first two parts of this special book. The first part tells us what the Lord said to the Prophet Moses when he lived on the earth.

The second part was translated from
ancient writings. A man named Mr.
Chandler found ancient records buried
with a mummy in Egypt. He heard that
Joseph Smith could translate ancient
writings so he brought the records to
Kirtland, Ohio. Joseph Smith was able to
translate them. They were writings from
the Prophet Abraham.

Along with these two writings, Joseph included the testimony of the disciple Matthew, the Articles of Faith and Joseph Smith's own personal history. These writings together are called The Pearl of Great Price.

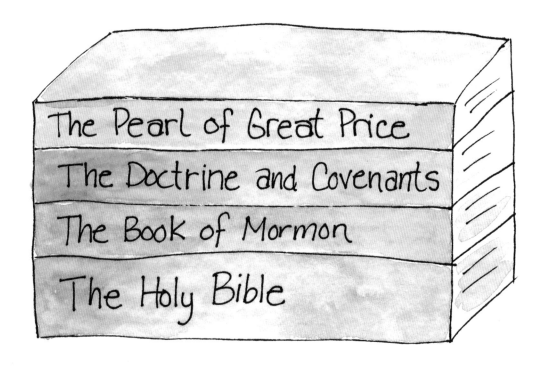

The Pearl of Great Price

The Doctrine and Covenants

The Book of Mormon

The Holy Bible

Early Church members used these writings along with The Book of Mormon, The Bible and The Doctrine and Covenants. Together, the four books are called The Standard Works. Today, Church members all around the world use the Standard Works and they can be found in many languages.

WARDS AND STAKES

Many people joined the Church during this time. After they joined, they wanted to move to Nauvoo to be with other Church members. People came from all over the world. Soon Nauvoo was a bustling city.

To accommodate all of the people at
church, Joseph created *wards* and
stakes. A ward is the name of a
congregation of people. Each ward has a
Bishop and other leaders. They worship
together on Sundays and they take care
of each other.

A stake is a larger group. A stake has several wards in it. While wards meet on Sunday, a stake meets only a few times a year. Both ward and stake leaders are aware of the needs of all the people in their area. If a person has a problem, the Church leaders can provide help.

AGUE
1839

The settlers built Nauvoo next to the Mississippi River. They drained the swampy wetland along the river's shore. Along with the river came mosquitoes. The mosquitoes were especially bad in the heat of the summer. Because most of the people worked outside they could not avoid being bitten by the mosquitoes.

While settling Nauvoo, a terrible disease tormented the Church members. The disease was called ague and mosquitoes may have caused it. Today, this disease is known as malaria.

A person with this disease feels burning hot and then freezing cold. It is a very uncomfortable disease. Ague swept through Nauvoo. Nearly everyone came down with it. Even Joseph Smith suffered from ague.

One day, the Prophet Joseph was tired
of feeling ill. He stood up and healed
himself with the power of the priesthood.
Then he blessed his family and Church
members who lived nearby. That day,
Joseph and many other Church
members were immediately healed.

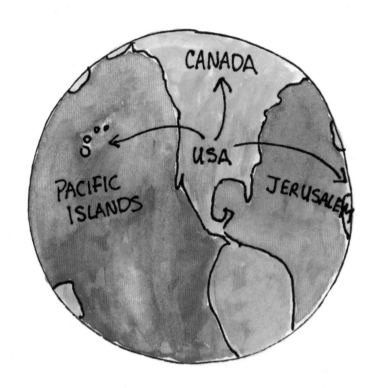

MISSIONARIES GO ABROAD
1839

During this time in Nauvoo, the Prophet called several men to serve missions. They traveled to Jerusalem, Canada, and the Pacific Islands. Others stayed in the United States. Many of the men had not fully recovered from ague, but they wanted to serve the Lord so they went anyway.

Two companions, Brigham Young and
Heber C. Kimball, were called on
missions while they were ill. Their
families were sick, too. The men felt bad
leaving sick family members behind.
Heber C. Kimball suggested to Brigham
Young that they wave good-bye to their
families.

As their wagon reached the top of a nearby hill, they stood up and shouted to their families, *"Hurrah, Hurrah, for Israel."* Three times they shouted this while waving their hats above their heads.

Their wives found the strength to stand up. They walked to their doorways and shouted back, *"Good-bye, God bless you."*

Because of the missionaries' hard work and sacrifice, lots of people joined the Church. The new converts wanted to live where other Church members were living. Many people came together from Europe, Canada and other parts of America. The Church membership continued to grow and grow.

> *"Journal of Louisa Barnes Pratt," in* Heart Throbs of the West, *comp. Kate B. Carter, 12 vols. (1939–51), 8:229*

A MOTHER'S FAITH
1839

Many husbands served missions. While the men were away, their families faced many challenges. Louisa Barnes Pratt faced a difficult time alone. Her daughter became ill with small pox. This is a very contagious disease and can cause death.

Louisa did not want anyone else to get the disease. She prayed to the Lord for help. Louisa prayed that her daughter would get well. She had faith that the Lord could do this.

After she prayed, her daughter felt better
and she only had a few pox marks. Later
on, a man came by their home. He was
familiar with the disease. He looked at
her pox marks. He said that she did
have the disease but that she was cured
by her mother's faith.

THE MARTYRDOM
27 JUNE 1844

Unfortunately, the Church members only enjoyed peace for a short time in Nauvoo. Many people did not like the new church. The Prophet knew he would soon die. Several times he told people that someday his enemies would take his life.

One day, he received a note from
Thomas Ford, the governor of Illinois.
The governor told the Church leaders to
come at once to stand trial. They were
charged with disturbing the peace. The
governor promised that they would be
protected while waiting for a fair trial.

Joseph left Nauvoo. He knew it was the last time he would ever see his family and friends. As he left Nauvoo, Joseph said, *"I am going like a lamb to the slaughter, but I am calm as a summer's morning."* His brother, Hyrum, went with him. John Taylor and other leaders followed him as well.

Joseph and three other Church leaders were put in the Carthage Jail. Governor Ford did not keep his promise. Two days later, two hundred mob members stormed the jail. The mob had painted faces and guns. They shot into the jail. Joseph, Hyrum and John Taylor were shot. Joseph and Hyrum died. John Taylor was wounded.

Willard Richards was also in the room. He was the only man not hit. He heard someone in the mob yell, *"The Mormons are coming!"* Then the mob ran away. Shortly after the shootings, a group of Joseph's friends arrived. They found their fallen Prophet. It was a very, very sad day for the Saints.

History of the Church, 6:555

BRIGHAM YOUNG
8 AUGUST 1844

Church members wondered who would be their next prophet. A large Church meeting was held. Several leaders stood to talk to the Saints. Brigham Young was one of the leaders. The people watching were very surprised when Brigham Young spoke. They said that Brigham Young looked and sounded just like Joseph Smith.

Wilford Woodruff commented, *"If I had not seen him with my own eyes, there is no one that could have convinced me that it was not Joseph Smith."* The Church members felt this was a sign from God. They believed Brigham Young was to be the next prophet. They united behind Brigham Young and the Church continued to grow in faith and numbers.

Quoted in History of the Church, 7:236

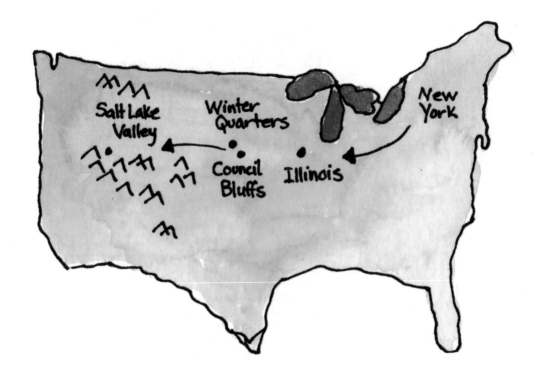

THE FIRST PIONEERS LEAVE NAUVOO
1846

For many years the Church leaders looked for a safe place to live. Once again, mean people came and the Saints were scared. Nauvoo was not safe anymore. The Church members prepared to follow Brigham Young. He knew of a safe place far, far away in the Rocky Mountains.

In those days, there were no cars or trains or airplanes. The people in Nauvoo had to make wagons and handcarts and prepare food to carry with them. The journey through the wilderness would take a long, long time.

They worked hard preparing for their
journey across the plains. They traveled
in groups. While traveling, they faced
many hardships.

Their first challenge was crossing the wide Mississippi River. The river was frozen during the winter. This made it especially challenging. The horses, cows and oxen were scared of the ice and did not want to cross over the frozen river. The people had to be very careful of soft spots where they might fall into the icy water.

After crossing the frozen river, the Saints crossed the flat plains of Iowa. This was very hard for most people. It was freezing cold outside. They had to sleep outside because they did not have proper tents or cabins to sleep in. Many people came down with illness during this part of the trip. Some even died.

WINTER QUARTERS

The Church members traveled
131 days from Nauvoo to a new
settlement. Here they would build cabins
and stay for the rest of the winter. They
called it Winter Quarters. This is near
present-day Omaha, Nebraska.

While most of the Saints planned to leave Winter Quarters in the spring, they planted crops anyway. This way, new Saints coming later on would have food to harvest in the late summer.

Over 3,500 people used Winter Quarters as their home during this time. It was not a pleasant place to be and the Saints were grateful when spring arrived. Now many of them could move on to the Rocky Mountains.

THIS IS THE RIGHT PLACE
1847

The pioneers traveled through the wilderness, hiking through plains and forests, crossing rivers with no bridges and climbing over hills and mountains. Some days were burning hot and some days were freezing cold.

At night, they set up tents and made
fires to cook their food and to stay
warm. Many times they finished the day
by singing together or dancing to fiddle
music. Some days were sad, but the
Saints tried to be happy.

From Winter Quarters, the journey lasted another 111 days. Brigham Young was in the first group to travel across the plains. Two men traveled ahead from this group to explore the Salt Lake Valley.

Orson Pratt and Erastus Snow found tall grass growing in the Salt Lake Valley. This was good news. This meant that other crops could grow well too. They also saw several fresh water creeks. The creeks would provide water for the people, their animals and their crops.

Three days later, Brigham Young crossed a mountain and approached the Salt Lake Valley for the very first time. He was very sick and was lying in the back of his wagon. He asked to have his wagon turned so that he could see the view.

Looking over the Salt Lake Valley, Brigham Young knew this was the place to stop. The Lord showed him this same valley in a dream before leaving Nauvoo. He was filled with joy. *"The spirit of light rested upon me and hovered over the valley, and I felt that there the Saints would find protection and safety."*

"It is enough. This is the right place."

To his group he said, *"It is enough. This is the right place."* What wonderful news for the Saints! Now they finally had a safe place to live. They were grateful to have a new home.

OUR HERITAGE: A Brief History of
The Church of Jesus Christ
of Latter-day Saints, 76

NOAH BRIMHALL

Some people could not leave Winter Quarters in the spring to travel to the Salt Lake Valley. They had to stay longer to collect money and supplies for the difficult journey. One young man who stayed behind was Noah Brimhall.

Noah first heard the gospel when he was fifteen years old. The next year Noah and two of his older brothers traveled to Nauvoo to see the Prophet Joseph Smith. However, Joseph was in jail in Illinois so they did not get to meet him. But they stayed in Nauvoo with the Church members and later moved on to Council Bluffs, Iowa.

Council Bluffs is located just across the river from Winter Quarters. Around 2,500 Saints lived in Council Bluffs while waiting to go west. Noah was baptized here in the Missouri River when he was twenty years old. He helped build 300 cabins for families who needed homes. He also helped build a ferry that carried people across the river between Council Bluffs and Winter Quarters.

During this time, Noah and his brother John found a paying job. They made wooden railroad ties out of big trees. The Quarter Master General at Ft. Laramie paid them $2.50 per hundred ties. After three years at Council Bluffs, the Brimhall brothers finally had the money and supplies needed to travel West. Noah was twenty-four years old when he left for the Salt Lake Valley.

Mildred Ann Rostrom Lewis,
The Story of Nellie Walker Rostrom

PRAYING FOR RAIN
1850

Noah Brimhall was so grateful. Soon he would leave Council Bluffs and move on to the Salt Lake Valley. However, just before leaving, he received bad news. It looked as if they might not be able to leave right away.

At a Church conference in the spring, Church leaders announced that the Plains were very dry. It had not rained for a long time. They could not travel under these conditions. At the conference an Apostle, Orson Hyde, asked the members to join him in prayer. He said that through their faith the Lord would send rain.

Together the congregation knelt down. They repeated the words of the Apostle. Fifteen minutes after praying, the rains came and extended across the Plains. As soon as the Saints heard the good news, they were filled with joy! They could leave as scheduled.

Noah and his group left on April 12th, 1850. They arrived in the Salt Lake Valley on July 27th. After three and one-half months of hard traveling through the wilderness they could finally stop. Noah and his brothers thanked the Lord for protecting them and bringing them safely to their new home.

Mildred Ann Rostrom Lewis,
The Story of Nellie Walker Rostrom

A GIFT FROM ENGLAND
1847

As the first pioneers were getting ready to leave Winter Quarters, several missionaries returned home. John Taylor returned from England. He had a special gift from the Church members living in England.

The English Saints sent tithing money to help the pioneers. They also sent useful scientific items to help in their travels. The money and the items helped the pioneers a lot. The gifts also showed their love and support for the pioneers.

ALL IS WELL
1847

Many pioneers followed the trail from Nauvoo to the Salt Lake Valley. Each person had his or her own story to tell. William Clayton was one of the first to travel to the Salt Lake Valley. He went ahead of his family and left his wife and her parents behind in Nauvoo.

William's wife was pregnant and expecting to deliver their first baby in one month. William thought about his wife a lot. He wondered if their baby had been born yet. He wondered if it was a boy or a girl, and he wondered if his wife and the baby were both okay.

William moved ahead each day wondering
how they were doing. Two months later, he
received news that his wife had delivered a
baby boy and that both were well. He was
so happy! He sat down and wrote a special
song. It explained how he and the other
pioneers felt.

He called his song, "Come, Come, Ye Saints." In the song he tells of the great trials the pioneers were facing. But he said that great joy followed their hardships. As his song says, *"All is well! All is well!"* During their many challenges the pioneers grew closer to God and felt His love. They found that after all the hardships that indeed . . . all is well!

James B. Allen, Trials of Discipleship: The Story of William Clayton, a Mormon *(1987), 202*

HANDCART PIONEERS
1856–60

After the first wagons came to the Salt Lake Valley, a new form of travel was created. The pioneers made handcarts that could be pulled by each person.

Handcarts are like wooden wagons, but
people pull them instead of oxen or
horses. The handcarts held everything
they owned. The handcarts were very
heavy and the pioneers had to pull them
over rocks and hills and across the
streams.

Ten different handcart groups left for the Salt Lake Valley. Eight of the ten groups made it safely there, but two groups ran into bad weather. Winter came early while they were still out on the Great Plains. They did not have shelter from the snow and wind. The pioneers were freezing cold. They also ran out of food early. It was very sad. Many people died in these two handcart groups.

A PIONEER'S TESTIMONY

A pioneer man in one of the fateful handcart groups survived. William Palmer said it was very hard crossing the Plains this way, but he felt it brought him closer to God. He wrote:

"I have pulled my handcart when I was
so weak and weary from illness and lack
of food that I could hardly put one foot
ahead of the other. I have looked ahead
and seen a patch of sand or a hill
slope and I have said, I can go only that
far and there I must give up, for I cannot
pull the load through it."

"I have gone on to that sand and when I
reached it, the cart began pushing me.
I have looked back many times to see
who was pushing my cart, but my eyes
saw no one. I knew then that the angels
of God were there."

"Was I sorry that I chose to come by handcart? No. Neither then nor any minute of my life since. The price we paid to become acquainted with God was a privilege to pay, and I am thankful that I was privileged to come in the Martin Handcart Company."

William Palmer, quoted in
David O. McKay, "Pioneer Women,"
Relief Society Magazine (Jan. 1948): 8

MORMON BATTALION
1846

One year, while the pioneers were crossing the Plains, a messenger caught up with them. He had a special request from the United States Government. The United States was at war with Mexico and the United States wanted the Mormons to help. They asked the men to join the army.

The Church leaders felt this would be a
good way to show their loyalty to the
United States. Also, the money they
earned could help the Saints. Brigham
Young believed the men would be safe.
He predicted that if they lived their
religion they would not have to fight and
no one would die.

A large group of pioneers volunteered to join the United States army. They were called the Mormon Battalion. Over 540 men marched to California to help in this cause. They had to march two thousand miles in the wilderness and desert with little food and water. It was very difficult.

On the way to California, the Mormon
Battalion marched through Tucson,
Arizona. Mexican soldiers were in the town.
When the Mexican soldiers saw the
Mormon Battalion marching toward them,
they were frightened. They thought they
would lose against such a large group of
soldiers.

The Mexican soldiers hid and the
Mormon Battalion marched through town
unharmed. The Mexicans then left
Tucson. Brigham Young had predicted
that the men would be safe and they
were. Not one man had to fight nor did
any die.

The Mormon Battalion fulfilled its one-year contract. After traveling so far away, the soldiers were grateful to finally return to their families and loved ones.

ABRAHAM HUNSAKER

One man who joined the Mormon
Battalion was Abraham Hunsaker. He left
his wife, Eliza Collins Hunsaker, and their
six young children to join the army.

   While away from his family, he worried
about them. He wondered if they were
healthy and safe. One night he had a
sad dream. He saw his wife and young
children suffering in their covered wagon
where he had left them.

They did not have telephones back then, and they could not even mail a letter, so Abraham had no way of knowing if they were all right. After his dream, he wondered if they were really suffering or if they were okay. Abraham prayed to Heavenly Father asking if they were okay.

The next morning while he was making breakfast, a white dove flew down and landed on Abraham's head. It only stayed for a moment but the other men noticed the dove. Abraham felt peace. He believed this was a sign from God that his family was safe and well.

The next morning, a white dove flew and circled around Abraham again and then flew away. The men commented, *"There's Hunsaker's dove!"* From then on, he felt peace knowing that his family was safe, and they were.

History of Abraham Hunsaker and His Family, *2d ed. (2001), 30–31*

THE *BROOKLYN*
1846

Most of the Saints traveled across the Great Plains to the Salt Lake Valley, but one group traveled a different way. They went by ship. This group of 238 Church members left from the New York harbor. They sailed on a ship called the *Brooklyn*.

Their voyage was difficult. They traveled
by sea for six months, and the ship was
small and crowded. Many people were
seasick. After a while, their food went
bad and they were hungry. A few people
died on the voyage, but along with the
hardships there were good times.

Two babies were born on the voyage.
Their parents named them Pacific and
Atlantic. Their names reflect the two
great oceans that they sailed. The
families were happy to welcome the
healthy new babies.

One time the ship stopped at a tropical island. Everyone got off and went on shore. They picked fresh fruit and potatoes. They were so glad to have clean water to bathe in and to drink. They washed their clothes in the clean water, too. They enjoyed five days of walking on solid ground and gathered food, water and supplies for the rest of the trip.

Finally, they landed in California. Some of the members stayed and settled in northern California. They named their settlement New Hope, but the rest of the Church members moved on to the Salt Lake Valley.

THE MIRACLE OF THE SEAGULLS
1848

The Salt Lake Valley was a refuge for the Saints. For the first time in many years, they finally had a safe place to live. They gave thanks to the Lord.

Land was divided up and the Saints built homes and churches. They also planted crops. They even planted extra crops for the new people coming. This way, everyone would have food.

One day, the farmers noticed black crickets swarming over their fields. The crickets were eating their crops. The Saints tried everything to get rid of the crickets, but they would not go away. With the crickets destroying their crops, they would not have any food to eat.

The Church members set a special date to fast and pray. They asked the Lord for help. Soon after praying, flocks of seagulls flew into the Valley. The seagulls flew over the crops and started eating the crickets. The Saints could hardly believe it! The seagulls saved their crops. The Lord answered their prayers and the Saints were so grateful.

NEW SETTLEMENTS

Soon the Salt Lake Valley began to flourish. Homes were built, farms were producing food, and a temple was being built. The people were grateful to have a safe new home in the West.

Around this time, Brigham Young started
calling families to move from their new
homes and settle new areas. He made
the announcements in General
Conferences. During the meetings,
President Young called out a family's
name. Then he assigned them an area
to settle.

The families felt this was a mission call. They brought all of their belongings to the new area. It was very hard to move again, but they chose to serve the Lord. The families built homes and planted crops.

The new settlements covered a large area. Settlements lined up and down the Salt Lake Valley. Some continued north into Idaho and Canada. Others continued south into Arizona, Nevada, and California.

SETTLING ARIZONA

One year at General Conference, a pioneer named Noah Brimhall was asked to settle in Arizona. He and his family packed their belongings and started their journey south. Other families were called to go as well. At one point, they had to cross the Big Colorado River.

It was winter, and the river was partly covered in ice. Noah said, "*We will try to cross the river when it is frozen.*" Mr. Johnson was surprised. He ran the ferry that crossed the river. He said, "*The Big Colorado doesn't freeze and has never been crossed that way.*" But Noah said, "*We will pray for the ice to thicken.*"

As the sun rose the next day, Noah
found the river completely frozen. He
and the other pioneers quickly made
sleds. Everyone helped. They unloaded
the wagons and moved their belongings
to the sleds. Noah shouted, *"The Lord is
on our side."*

Crossing over the ice was so much fun
for the children. They raced happily back
and forth pulling the sleds. Now came
the hard part. They had to get their
animals to the other side of the river. The
animals were scared and did not want to
cross the ice. They would not move at
all.

"*I have it,*" shouted a man with a basket of sand. He began throwing the sand over the slick ice. He made a sandy trail for the animals to cross over.

The old mare went first. She was the
leader, and the other animals always
followed her. Once the old mare crossed
the ice, all the others followed. *"Now for
the wagons with all speed,"* shouted a
pioneer as he noticed the sun getting
warmer.

The white hooded wagons moved
slowly but surely over the ice. One by
one, each wagon landed safely on the
shore. As the last team stepped onto the
firm ground, a loud cracking noise rang
out. The ice broke and the back wheels
of the wagon went down into the water,
but the loyal team of oxen pulled it
safely to land.

"Then the pioneers went on their way," wrote one family member, "Singing praises to their Lord, who had truly been with them. This was the first and last time the Colorado River was ever crossed on ice in that place."

Mildred Ann Rostrom Lewis,
The Story of Nellie Walker Rostrom

WILLIAM WALKER

Many blessings came to those who helped settle new areas. A man named William Albert Walker helped settle Arizona. He told of several times when he was blessed.

The Apache tribe was the local Indian
group in this area. Once in awhile, the
Indians went on the warpath. This meant
that they attacked the people living in the
area. They burned down houses, stole
horses and killed people they did not
know.

William worked as an Indian scout. He watched out for the Indians. When they were on the warpath, he warned his family and friends.

One evening, William was camping out
at nearby White Mountain. He put out his
campfire and was lying under a tree. He
had a strong impression that he should
get up and move. He moved away with
his horses and found another place to
sleep.

Just as he was getting comfortable, he
saw Indians coming in his direction. He
placed his hands over his horse's nose
to keep it quiet. One horse was trained
to never make a sound when Indians
were near, but his other horse needed
help to be quiet. William waited like this
for two hours!

The Indians looked around where he had been earlier. Some of the Indians even came over to his old campfire and kicked the ashes. William was grateful that he was inspired to move. After the Indians left, he fell asleep and was safe for the rest of the night.

Mildred Ann Rostrom Lewis,
The Story of Nellie Walker Rostrom

THE LITTLE BIBLE

One day, several Apache Indians surrounded William Walker. He was out scouting when they happened to see him first. The Indians started moving in and circled around him. But then, William said, the strangest thing happened.

Suddenly, a man came out of nowhere. He handed William a little Bible. The man said that he should carry it over his heart all the time. The Indians then started to back off and left William alone.

William started carrying the little Bible in his shirt pocket everywhere he went. One day that little Bible helped save him again.

Once, William was out scouting for Indians and was shot by a gun. The bullet went into his chest but William was not harmed. He was carrying the little Bible in his shirt pocket. The bullet lodged into the Bible and it protected William. The bullet did not even touch his skin! William was amazed and thankful for this little Bible that saved his life.

Mildred Ann Rostrom Lewis,
The Story of Nellie Walker Rostrom

BRIGHAM YOUNG'S LEGACY

Brigham Young was a great leader. In the early years in the Salt Lake Valley, he wanted to meet every new member. He made sure that everyone had a place to live. He also helped the people find jobs. Because of his compassion and humor, the Saints loved him.

In thirty years' time, Brigham Young took
a lonely desert and developed it into a
thriving community, Salt Lake City. He
founded over two hundred towns. He
established a government and built
factories and schools. Encouraging the
Saints to enjoy life, he promoted art,
drama and music.

Brigham Young taught by example. He
was a hardworking man and wanted all
the Saints to keep busy doing good
things. Within his own home, he used
wood carved beehives as decorations.
They were to remind his family members
to keep busy just like the bees that
surround a beehive.

Brigham Young was especially dedicated to the Church. He once said, *"My whole life is devoted to the Almighty's service."* Brigham Young was the prophet for thirty-three years before passing away from an illness. Church members will always remember him for his compassion, vision of the future and for leading the Saints to a safe land.

Quoted in Gordon B. Hinckley,
Truth Restored (1979), 127–28

A NEW PROPHET

After Brigham Young died, the Lord chose a new prophet to lead the Church. His name was John Taylor. The Saints were grateful to have a living prophet. They supported him by following the commandments and by doing what was right.

Wilford Woodruff was the fourth prophet
and president of the Church. Next came
Lorenzo Snow. President Snow taught
the law of tithing. Every Church member
gives ten percent of what they earn to
the Church. The Church uses tithing
money to build new churches and
temples and to help build the church.

Joseph F. Smith was the next prophet.
President Smith saw a busy, changing
world and he was concerned about the
Church members. He asked the Saints to
have *Family Home Evening* each week.
By setting aside time to be with family,
he believed families would stay close to
each other and close to the Lord.

Following Joseph F. Smith came Heber J. Grant, George Albert Smith, David O. McKay, Joseph Fielding Smith and Harold B. Lee. President Lee started the Welfare program. This program helps people who need food and clothes. Next came Spencer W. Kimball, Ezra Taft Benson, Howard W. Hunter and Gordon B. Hinckley.

Each new prophet leads the Church
members just as Joseph Smith and
Brigham Young once did. The prophet
gives counsel and guidance to the
Saints. There are millions of Church
members now. They live in all parts of
the world and speak all sorts of
languages. All of the members look to
the president of the Church for spiritual
direction.

THE SALT LAKE TEMPLE
6 APRIL 1893

In 1893, the Saints were so happy. After forty years of hard work, the Salt Lake Temple was finally finished! All of the Saints had worked very hard. Some artists were sent on a mission to Europe to study with the world's best artists. They brought their new skills back to Utah to make the Salt Lake Temple a beautiful place.

The Saints felt unity on this special day. After years of hardship and disappointment, they felt this was a turning point. The Saints' lives were improving. They had food, clothing, shelter, and could work, study and worship in peace. The dedication of the Salt Lake Temple was truly a joyful day.

Since the dedication of the Salt Lake Temple, many other temples around the world have been completed. Temples are very special.

Just three years after Joseph Smith organized the church in 1830, the first temple was started. The Lord commanded, ". . . *build a house unto me . . . establish a house, even a house of prayer, a house of fasting, a house of faith, a house of learning, a house of glory, a house of order, a house of God.*"

Couples go to the temple to be married
forever. New families joining the Church
go to the temple to be sealed together
forever as a family. People feel very
special when they are inside the temple.
The temple is a sacred and holy place.

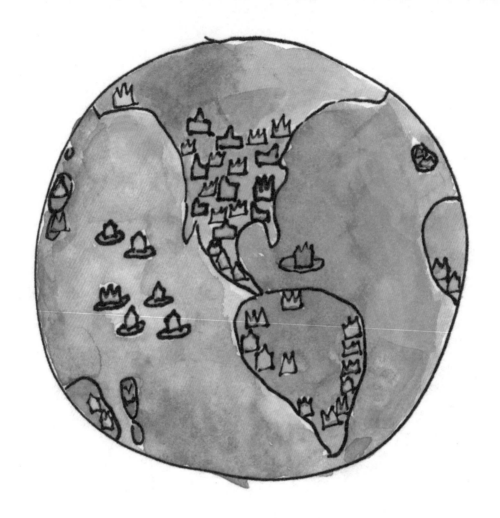

There are over one hundred temples around the world now. Church members are grateful to have temples near their homes so they can go often to worship and to feel God's love.

Doctrine and Covenants 109:8

A LITTLE VOICE

Heavenly Father blesses people who go to the temple. Miracles and good things seem to surround the temple. Many people tell of experiences where the temple has brought them peace.

One day, not so long ago, a young
couple was expecting their first baby.
The mother-to-be went to see her doctor.
The doctor said that the baby might
have a problem. He thought the baby
had stopped growing.

The doctor wanted pictures taken of the baby inside the mother. This is called an ultrasound. The doctor could look at the pictures and tell if something was wrong. He scheduled the ultrasound for that day, but unfortunately, it was Friday and the ultrasound could not be read until Monday. That was in three days!

The mother was very worried. She was
afraid that her baby was not healthy. She
called her father and told him about the
situation. Her father was worried, too.
The next day he went to the Seattle
Temple. At the temple, he prayed for his
daughter and her unborn baby.

He felt peace in the temple. After praying, he heard a little sweet voice. It said, *"I'm okay."* He went home feeling sure that the baby was healthy. He called his daughter and told her not to worry. Monday morning the doctor read the ultrasound. He told the mother, *"Your baby is growing and will be fine."*

The baby was born a few weeks later. It was a girl! Her parents named her Amanda and loved her very much. She was healthy and just the right size.

The mother called her parents to tell them that she had had a baby girl. When her father heard the news, he said, "*Just in case I was wrong, I didn't want to say anything earlier, but I was the first to know it was a girl. The voice I heard in the temple was that of a little girl.*"

Personal Story of Loren Milam Blocher and Laura Lee Blocher Rostrom

JOY TO THE WORLD!

The Church of Jesus Christ of Latter-day Saints continues to grow. Missionaries are teaching the gospel to people all around the world. They share the Book of Mormon with people who want to learn more. Many people are grateful to hear about the Church.

On a rainy day in Olympia, Washington,
Ellis and Edith Blocher met Church
members for the very first time. The
couple wanted to hear more about the
Mormon Church. They received a Book
of Mormon and promised to read it.

The couple wanted to find the true
Church of Jesus Christ. They believed
they found what they were looking for
after reading the Book of Mormon twice.
In 1942, they were baptized and joined
the Church along with their four children.

Their youngest child, Loren, was nine years old. He remembers going to Church for the first time. They met at a member's home. There were only three other families. When Loren and his family walked into Church, the people were so happy! The small group nearly doubled with the Blocher's family of six!

The ELLIS BLOCHER FAMILY 1942

Ellis and Edith enjoyed watching their family embrace the Church. Their children later married other Church members. Soon they had twenty grandchildren and eventually over sixty great-grandchildren. They were so thankful for the gospel and for the family who first shared it with them.

The happiness that the Blochers received from joining the Church did not stop there. It has been passed down to their grandchildren and great-grandchildren. This joy is available to all who want it. Hard working missionaries and Church members share the gospel with others, bringing joy to the world!

Personal story by Loren Milam Blocher and Leona Blocher Betteridge

FEED MY SHEEP

Jesus had twelve disciples when he lived on the earth. One day, Jesus asked Simon Peter, " *'Lovest thou me?' He saith unto him, Yea, Lord; thou knowest that I love thee. He saith unto him, 'Feed my sheep.'* " Jesus asked Simon Peter this same question three times. Every time, Jesus taught him, *"Feed my sheep."*

Do you think Jesus really wanted Simon Peter to feed sheep? No. He was asking him to teach people about the gospel. He wanted him to teach others so they would not be hungry spiritually. Jesus was asking Simon Peter to be a missionary.

Shortly after Joseph Smith organized the Church, he left on a mission. He knew it was important. Latter-day Saints believe that Jesus still wants his followers to tell people about the gospel. That is why The Church of Jesus Christ of Latter-day Saints has missionaries serving all over the world.

Jesus Christ is the foundation of the Church. All members want to be like Him. They try to choose the right so they will be able to live with Him again. From the earliest Church members up until now, all want the same thing. They look forward to the day when they will return to live with Heavenly Father and Jesus. That will be a wonderful day!

St. John 21:15–17

IMPORTANT CHURCH EVENTS

1820
The First Vision

1829
Priesthood
Restored

1830
The Book of
Mormon
Published

The Church of
Jesus Christ of
Latter-day Saints
Restored

1831
Saints Leave
New York

1833
Word of
Wisdom
Given

1836
Kirtland
Temple
Dedication

1838–39
Saints Leave
Missouri and
Settle in Nauvoo

1842
Relief Society
Begins

1844
Joseph Smith
Killed

Brigham
Young
Becomes
Second
Prophet of
the Church

1847
Brigham
Young Enters
the Salt Lake
Valley

Pioneers
Follow

1877
Brigham
Young Dies
of Illness

John Taylor
Becomes Third
Prophet of the
Church

1893
Salt Lake
City
Temple
Dedicated

ABOUT THE
AUTHOR/ILLUSTRATOR

Laura Lee Blocher Rostrom is a native of Seattle, Washington, and is a graduate of Brigham Young University. She currently lives in Westchester County, New York, with her husband, Dean, and their three children.